Look a
Me!

Written by Trevor Hudson

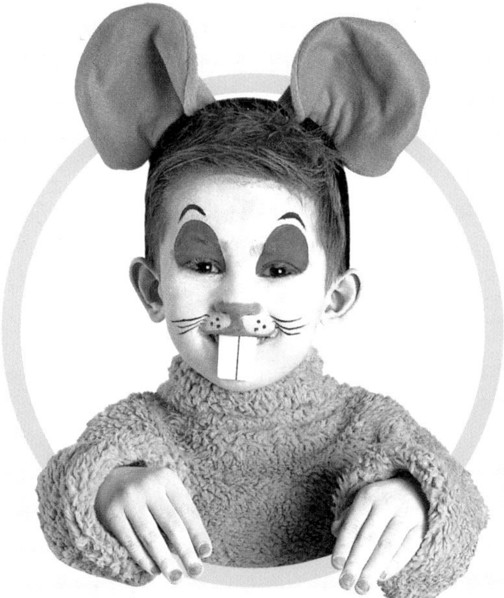

Look at me.

I am a mouse.

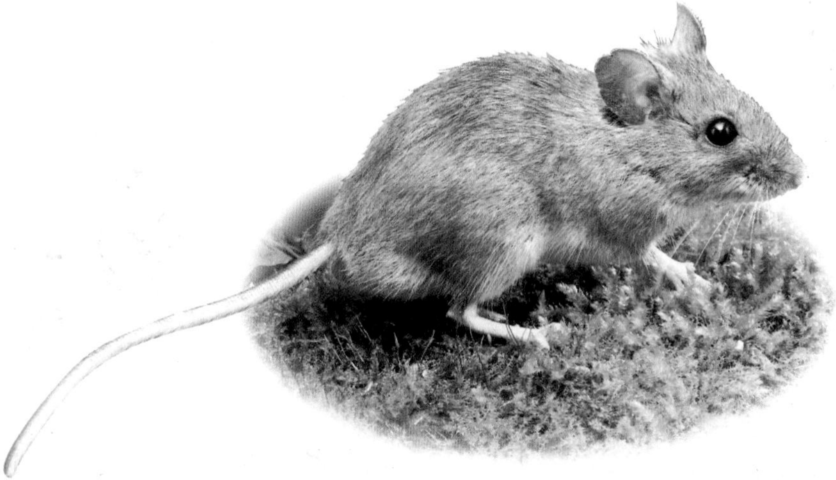

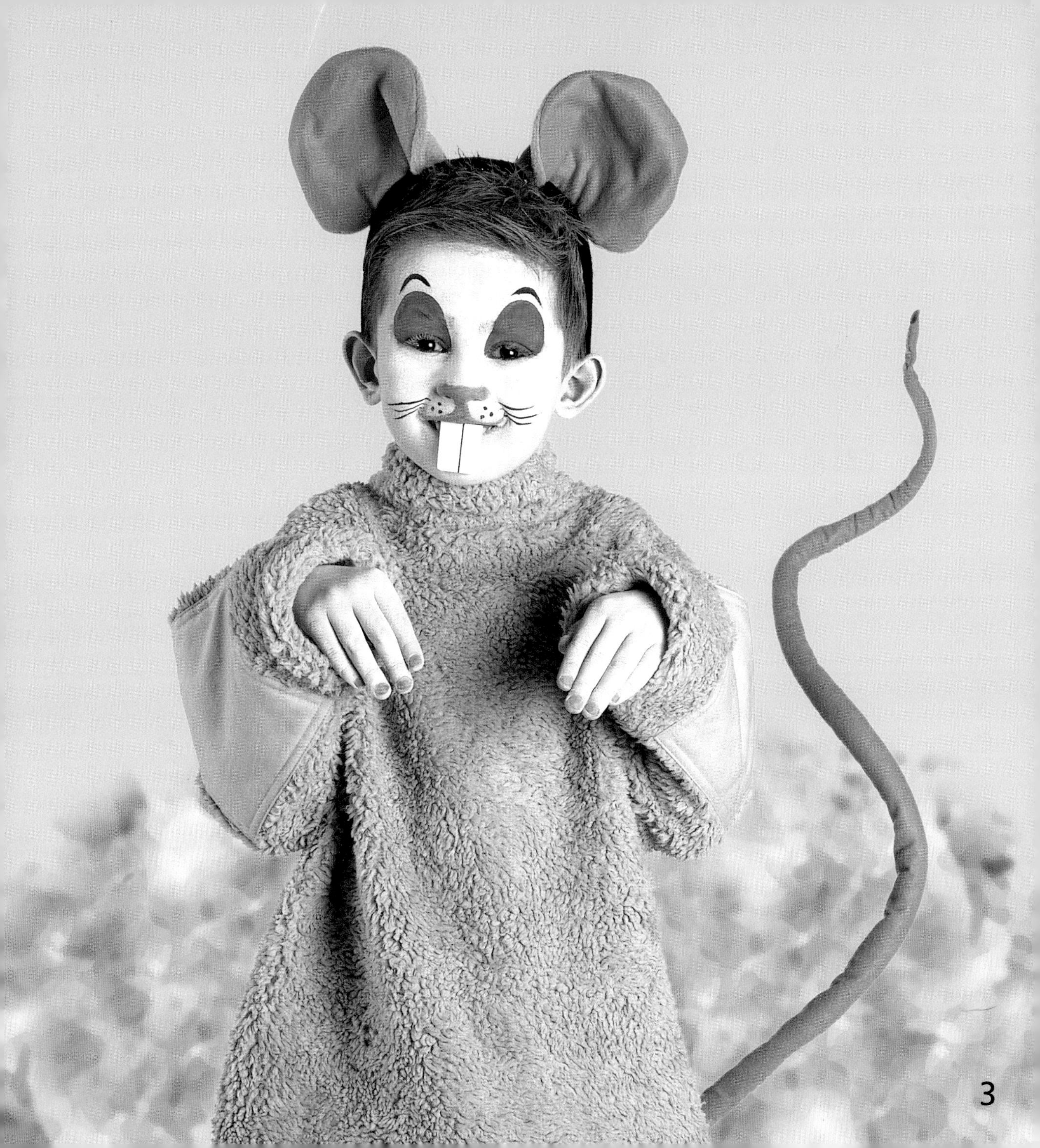

Look at me.
I am a frog.

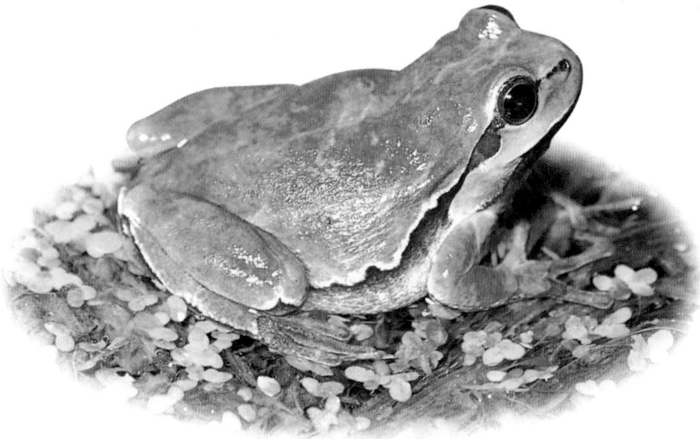

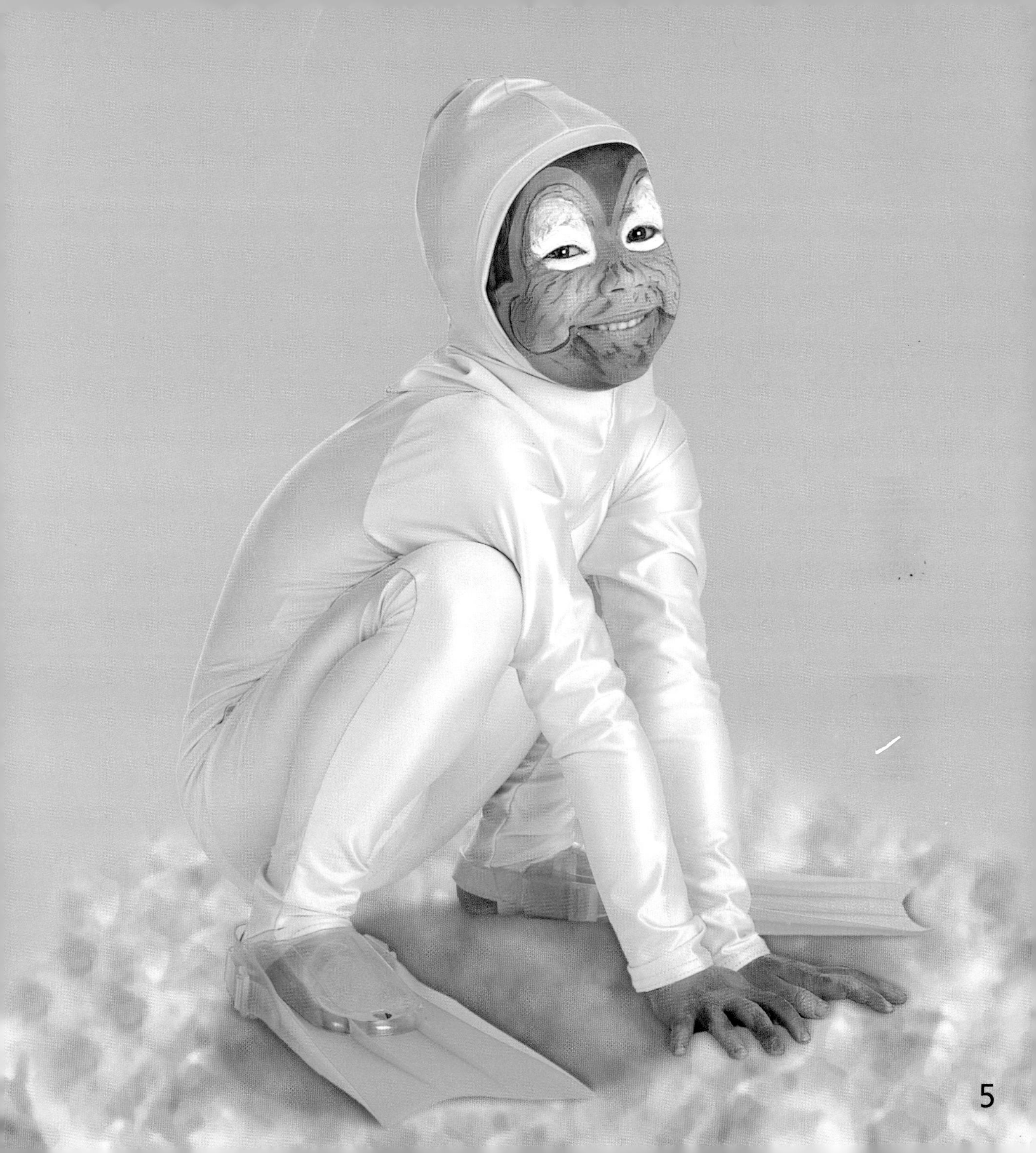

Look at me.

I am a rabbit.

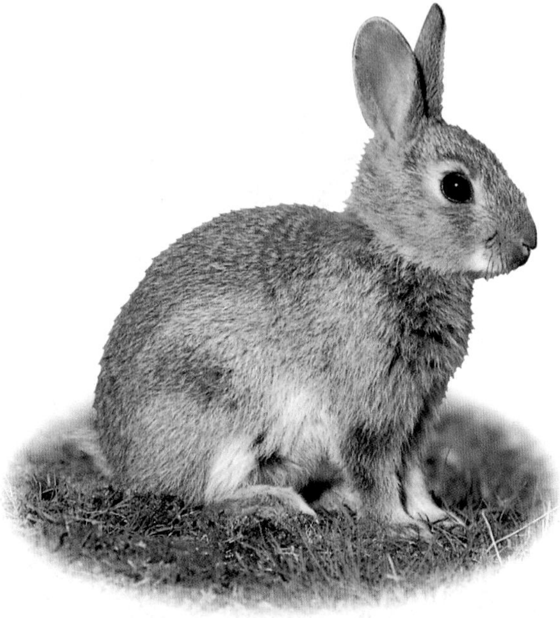

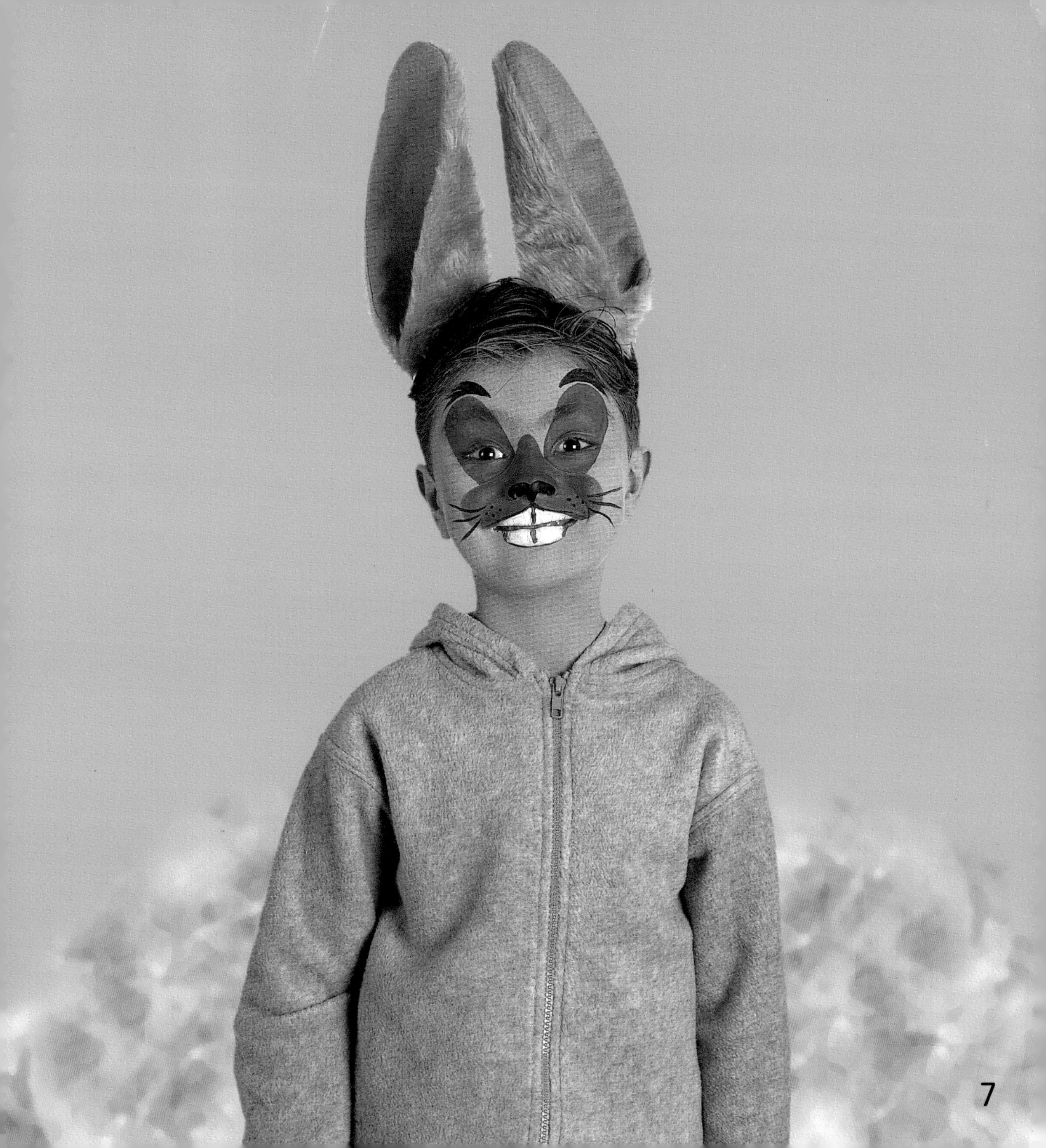

Look at me.

I am a chicken.

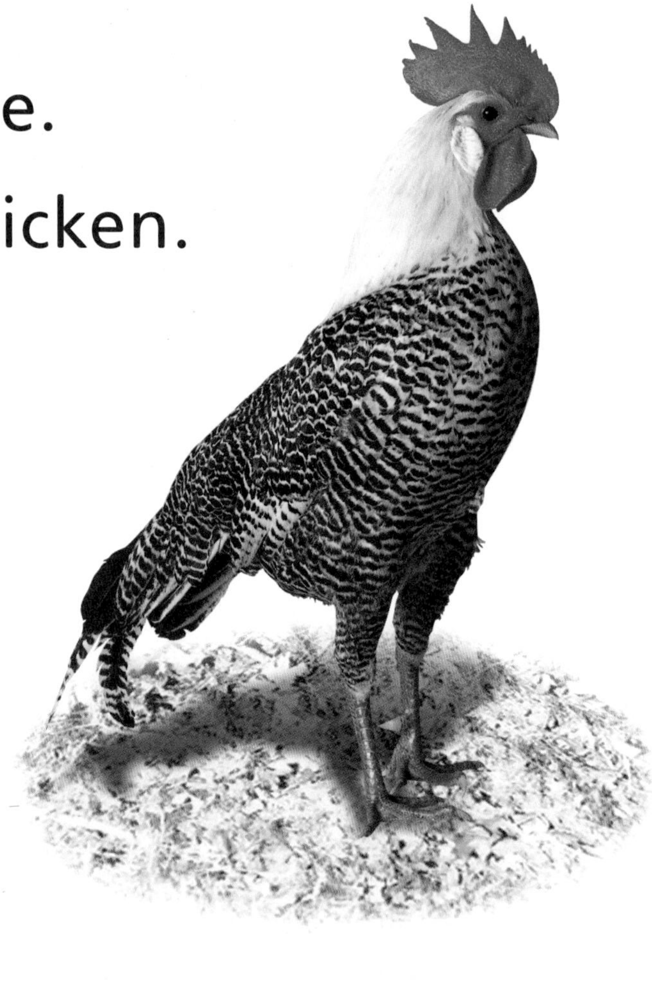

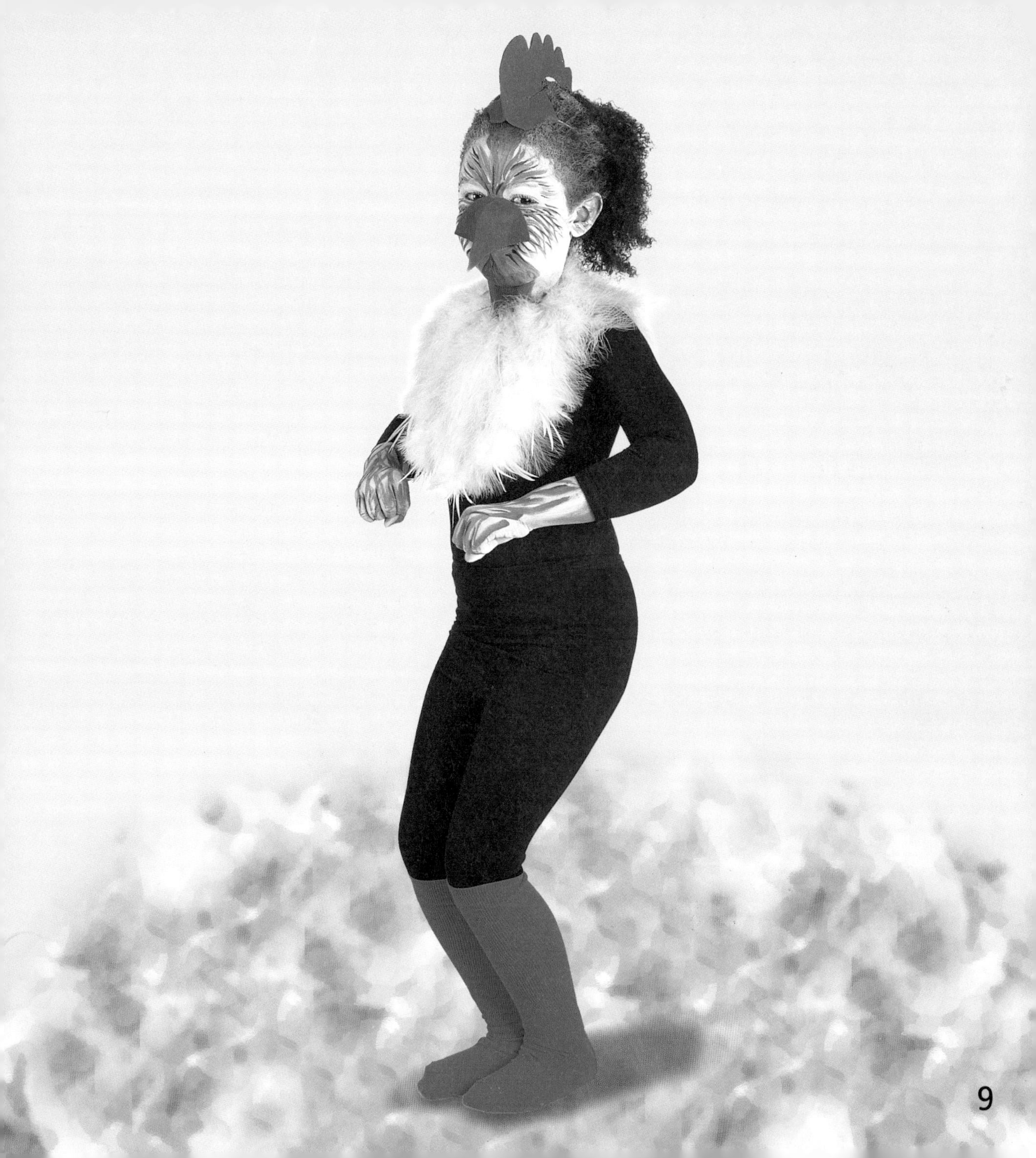

Look at me.
I am a fox.

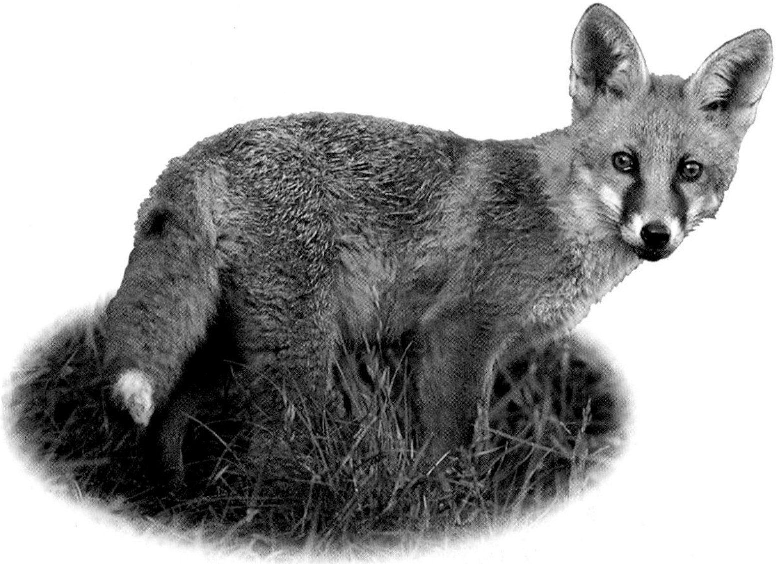

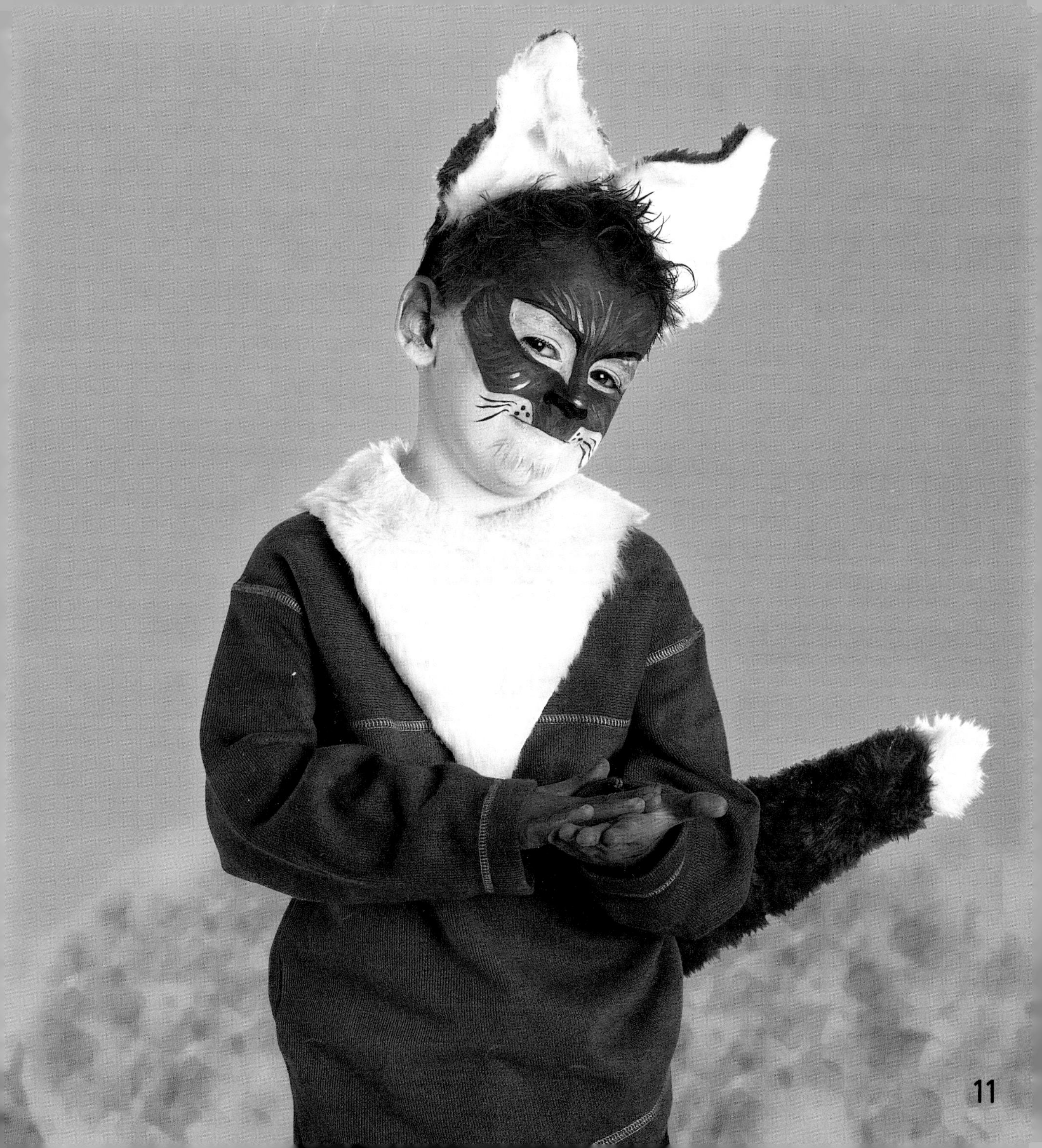

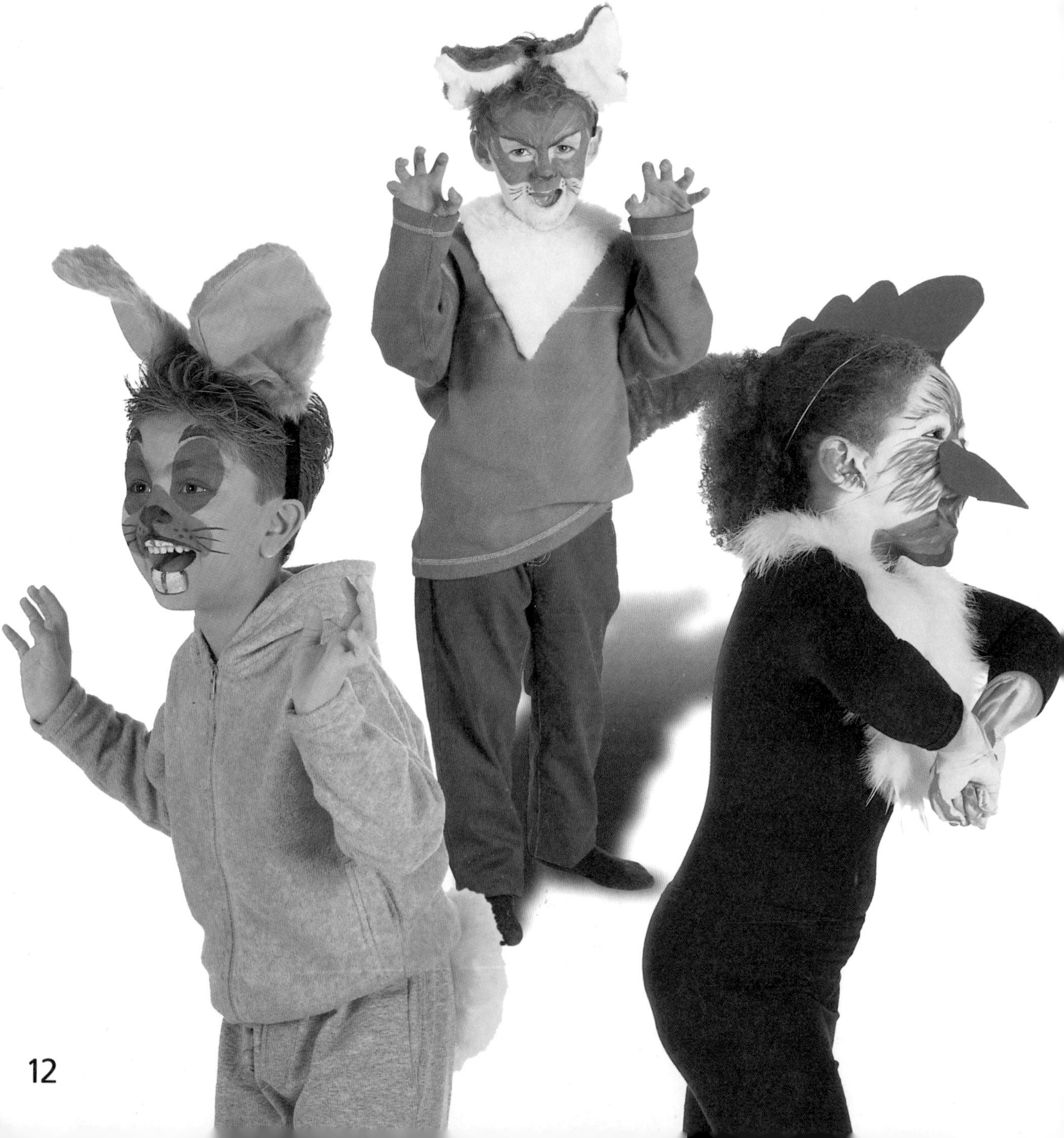